For
Oliver

First published 2024 by Walker Books Ltd, 87 Vauxhall Walk, London SE11 5HJ

This edition published 2025

2 4 6 8 10 9 7 5 3 1

© 2024 Catherine Rayner

The right of Catherine Rayner to be identified as author of this work has been asserted
in accordance with the Copyright, Designs and Patents Act 1988

EU Authorized Representative: HackettFlynn Ltd, 36 Cloch Choirneal, Balrothery, Co. Dublin, K32 C942, Ireland. EU@walkerpublishinggroup.com

This book has been typeset in Baskerville

Printed in China

British Library Cataloguing in Publication Data: a catalogue record for this book
is available from the British Library

ISBN 978-1-5295-2315-7

www.walker.co.uk

WALKER BOOKS
AND SUBSIDIARIES
LONDON · BOSTON · SYDNEY · AUCKLAND

Molly, Olive & Dexter
You Can't Catch Me!
Catherine Rayner

At the bottom of the garden, there's an oak tree.

It's home to Molly the hare, Olive the owl and Dexter the fox.

Dexter LOVES chasing games.
"Come on," he says to his friends, "let's play!"
Olive isn't looking, so Dexter touches her
wing with his nose. "You're it, Olive!"

"And you can't catch me…"

says Molly.

"We'll see about that!" Olive circles through the air, and before Molly can get very far, she swoops down to touch her ear.

"Now YOU'RE it, Molly!"

She hoots and they all giggle.

Dexter races off. He hears Molly's feet thumping
after him, and just as she gets close … he spins
round and chases in the other direction!
"You can't catch me!" he cries.

But Molly is SO fast! She races up
to Dexter by the oak tree. They go
round the trunk in a circle,
but things get all in
a muddle: now Molly
is ahead of Dexter …

and before long …

BUMP!

"Got you!" Molly laughs,
and off she whizzes again.

Now Dexter is all dizzy,
and he can't seem to catch
either of his friends.

When he nearly reaches Molly,

she darts and leaps away.
She's just too quick!

When he's close to Olive, she swoops and swerves off. She's just too clever at flying!

"You can't catch us," they call, "and we're going to WIN this game."

Poor Dexter is all worn out from chasing. What now?
He doesn't have wings like an owl. He doesn't have
big strong feet like a hare.

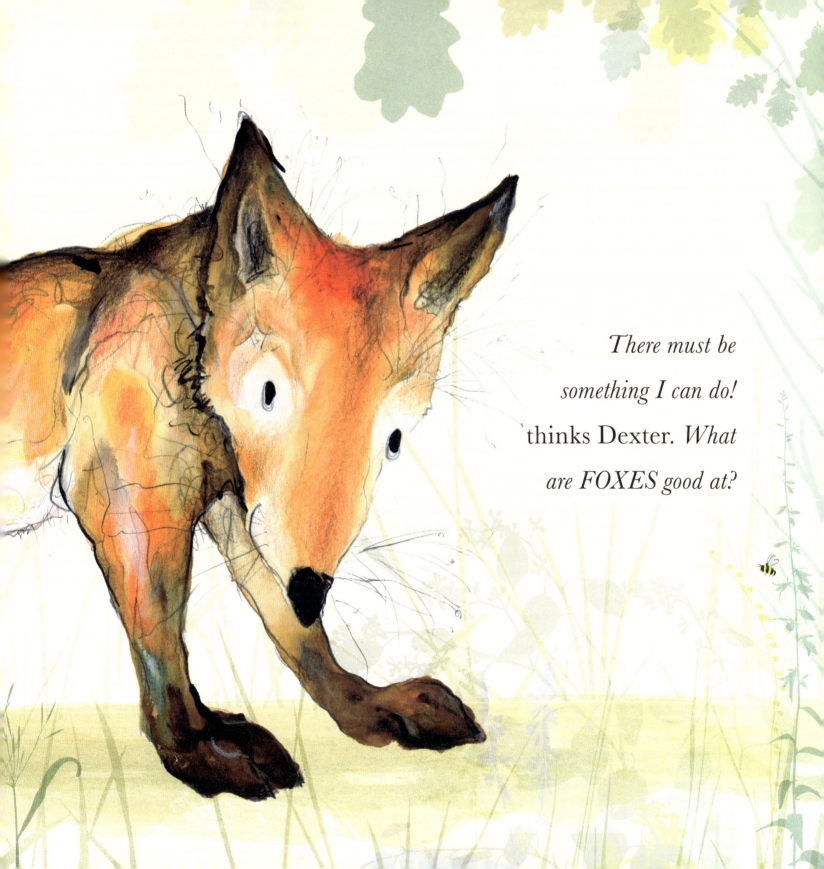

*There must be
something I can do!*
thinks Dexter. *What
are FOXES good at?*

Now Olive and Molly are very puzzled.

"Where has Dexter gone?" asks Olive.

"He was here one second ago!" says Molly.

Olive flies up high, looking for clues.
Molly looks down low, checking in
all her favourite hiding places.

"He's disappeared!" says Molly, coming

to rest on the big pile of leaves.

"Oh dear," says Olive, perching beside her.

"Maybe he didn't like losing."

But all of a sudden …

"BOO!"

Out jumps Dexter in

a flurry of leaves.

"You're it, Molly! You're
it, Olive!" he cries.
"Got you both in one."

"Oh, Dexter!" Olive hoots.

"That was a very good plan."

"How did you think of that?"

says Molly. "You're so clever."

"That's what foxes do," says Dexter, looking very proud.

"I'm not as quick as Molly, and I can't fly like Olive – but

I can think of clever plans!"

"Well done, Dexter," says Molly. "You win!"

"But that's not quite true." Dexter smiles. "We **ALL** won,

didn't we?" He gives his friends a great big hug…

And before long they settle under the oak tree

at the bottom of the garden for a nice long nap.

Three best friends.